"... missable" *SUNDAY TIMES*

"A story of few words, great heart and lingering impact" *GUARDIAN*

"Stunningly illustrated by Emma Shoard, this short story by the late Siobhan Dowd is full of sensitivity and subtle, deft storytelling, and reminds readers of the need for compassion and understanding" BOOKTRUST

"Has all the hallmarks of [Dowd's] later novels – sparse, clear but lyrical language; a clear and intuitive insight into the hearts and souls of young people; unflinching in its lack of sentimentality while still being deeply moving" THE BOOKBAG

"The sheer depth and emotion packed into this spare narrative is still breath-taking. This is a book to treasure" ANDREA REECE

"Siobhan Dowd worked for the rights of Travellers and her book gives real insight into their lives, not just the prejudice they endure, but the warmth and closeness of their communities. At a time when hostility to those regarded as 'other' or outsiders seems almost entrenched in society, this powerful, beautifully told story seems ever more important" BOOKS FOR KEEPS

First published in 2017 in Great Britain by
Barrington Stoke Ltd
18 Walker Street, Edinburgh, EH3 7LP

www.barringtonstoke.co.uk

This edition first published 2019

Text © 2004 Siobhan Dowd
Illustrations © 2017 Emma Shoard

This story was first published in an anthology of stories,
Skin Deep (Penguin Books Ltd, 2004)

A CIP catalogue record for this book is available
from the British Library upon request

ISBN: 978-1-78112-879-4

Printed in Malaysia by Times Offset

SIOBHAN DOWD

the PAVEE

and the BUFFER

GIRL

illustrated by
Emma Shoard

Barrington Stoke

"As a writer, Dowd appears to be incapable of a jarring phrase or a lazy metaphor. Her sentences sing, each note resonates with an urgent humanity of the sort that cannot be faked" *GUARDIAN*

FOREWORD

Many years ago, the author and editor Tony Bradman approached a contact he knew from the campaigning writers' organisation PEN to ask for recommendations of writers who might contribute a story about Traveller children to an anthology on racism. That contact was Siobhan Dowd, and she tentatively offered herself to write the story. "The Pavee and the Buffer Girl" would become her first published work.

In the words of Patrick Ness, Siobhan Dowd *"was a woman who worked for human rights charities, who set up the Siobhan Dowd Trust so that after her death the money her books earned would go to help children who needed it, a woman who wanted to tell this story so much, she offered herself – an unpublished writer – as a candidate."*

Patrick goes on to say, *"I don't think she wrote a story about Irish Traveller children because she wanted to preach to us. I think the story burned within her. And I think the reason it burned within her was because it was also an act of compassion, of empathy, an act – dare I say it? – of love."*

Siobhan's career was cut tragically short by her early death from cancer. The Trust she established in her last days continues the work of taking books to those who cannot access them, like Jim in this story, and his mam. You can find out more about the Trust at siobhandowdtrust.com.

"Don't go digging up troubles," his mam called as
he set off. "You and your da, you're the one pair.
Digging up troubles like bad old potatoes."

Jim turned back and waved, catching her in
a smile. Her old yellow frock flapped in the June

wind, matching the Calor gas bottles round the trailers.

"Aways with you," she said.

He went down the steep hill towards Dundray. As the morning haze thinned, he could make out the speckled dots of houses and a faint trace of the pier from the white shimmer of sea. Somewhere down there was the school. He'd have given anything not to go. But the education people had been around three times waving papers and mouthing the law, and his mam and da had given in.

"It'll only be a few weeks, Jimmy," his da said. "Then you can come scrapping again."

"The Buffers may be better down there," his mam said. "Try and get a few words of the reading off them."

In the last school, a year ago, he'd picked up a black eye and a bruised collarbone in two weeks, but no reading. The thought of all those books with the ugly black marks like secret codes was worse than all the fights put together. He paused, wondering if he should jump over the hedge and run for it, but his uncle Mirt pulled up behind him in the van.

"Are yous off down that Buffer school too?" he said.

"S'pose."

"Hop in. I'll drop you at the gate with the others."

He climbed in the back where his cousins crouched, their faces dropping to the South Pole.

"I've never bin to secondary school before," said young Declan. He wheezed with the asthma and took out his spray.

"It's the pits," said May. Lil mimed a doom-laden spit.

"It's worse than the pits," said Jim. "Give me a mine to go down any day."

"What's it like so, Jimmy, if it's worse than the pits?" said Declan.

"It's like a laboratory run by robots. And we're the rats. The ones they give electric shocks to as an experiment." The van lurched over a hump in the road and came to a stop. "And it smells like a bit of cheese from the last century – any decent rat would turn up its nose."

"We're here," said Uncle Mirt. "Out yous all get and no malarkying."

But he beckoned Jim over and whispered, "Would you ever keep an eye out for young Declan? The wheezing's been wicked bad of late." Jim nodded and followed the others through the school gates.

They stood in a line staring across the grounds at the huddles of maroon uniforms. Jim glanced towards Declan. He could hardly see his face for the freckles, but he could tell he was frightened from the way he stood so close. A gang lounging near the hurling hut drifted over. When they were within range, one of them said, "They look like brown smut. My dad says that's what they are."

"Whisht, they might put a curse on us," another hissed.

Jim felt like baring his teeth and crossing his two forefingers into a blasphemous crucifix, to give them something to think about. But his mam's "don't-go-digging-troubles" voice rang in his head.

He looked away, and found himself locked in a gaze with a different girl, who stood on her own. She was chubby, with bright high bunches. Her uniform was baggy, her socks down around her ankles. She half smiled, half shrugged at

him, and then stared upwards as if the whole school was a show.

He thought about stepping over to say hello, but as he put his foot forward, it was as if a force-field stopped him, his da telling him to keep away. "Don't go messing with any Buffers. They're all the same. They hate us Pavees. Do your business with them and walk away."

13

A bell rang. The school filed into the gym for assembly like maroon ants. Jim tried a devil-may-care saunter, miming a whistle, but all around the stares were coming at him, so he fixed his eyes to the linoleum and tried to vanish instead. He felt a right bad thumb in his old dark suit, however long his mam had pressed it.

Someone handed him a hymnbook and when everyone started singing about Love Divine coming down, he pretended to join in. He knew he

had the book the right way up; he'd learned that much. But he didn't know the right page, so he kept the book in a narrow crack, close to his nose. Then they filed out to various classrooms. In his, the form teacher was waiting, sitting back on his dais, tapping his pen on the register.

"You," he said. "Sit here." He indicated a vacant seat in the front row. It was next to the lone girl from the playground.

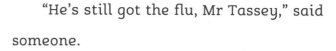

There was silence as the teacher looked around, marking off names in the register.

"Where's Leahy?" he said.

"He's still got the flu, Mr Tassey," said someone.

"It's a strange flu altogether," he said, "this summer flu. You, the new boy. Stand up and tell us who you are."

"Me?" said Jim.

"Who else?"

Jim stood up and looked around the class. There were smirks and boredom, curiosity, expectant shuffles.

"I'm me," he said at last. There were sniggers.

"Your name," said Mr Tassey. "You must know that much."

"Which one?" said Jim.

"All of them!"

"Only, sees, I was baptised six times. James Jonathan Jeremiah. Joseph Jacob Jonas. Curran. They call me Big J in camp. But Jim Curran's fine."

"Well, Jim Curran," said Mr Tassey. "Sit down and less blackguarding. Understood?"

He sat down, but when the teacher had turned his back he rolled his eyes around in their sockets. The girl next to him grinned. He caught her eye

and winked. She scribbled something on her exercise book and showed it to him. It was a cartoon of the teacher.

His big chin and nose poked out like Popeye's, and on his head was a lampshade with tassels hanging down. A talking balloon came out his mouth. Jim couldn't read what she'd written in it, but he guessed "Mr Tassel". He guffawed silently and she leaned towards him. "I'm Kit," she whispered, offering him a mint.

His mam said Purgatory was a waiting room, where souls howled for years remembering their evil deeds. School was worse. He could not follow the lessons, but he followed the movements from class to class, pretending he was the Invisible

Man. He sat near the window in Geography and followed the lawn-mowing sound out on the field.

In Maths he followed a line of stickmen scratched on to his wooden desktop, marching up to an old inkwell. He imagined them falling in and drowning, one after another.

Between classes he followed the corridors, trying to ignore the way older crowds jostled him. If he passed the younger ones, they parted before him like the Red Sea, as if he were a walking curse. He followed his fate to the next classroom, thinking of when he might go home.

"It's the tinker-stinker," he heard them say.

Time was like his da's old accordion. When you wanted to spin it out, it squashed up into a dashing quickstep. When you wanted it to pass, it stretched out into a long tuneless whine.

He came across Declan in the break.

"How's it going?" said Jim.

"I couldn't do the spelling test. I handed mine in with nothing on it."

"They made me write out a hundred lines once at the last place," Jim said. "I just handed in rows of waves and loops. And you know what?"

"What?"

"Nobody said anything. Perhaps *they* can't tell the difference either."

The first fight happened near the fish and chip shop by the pier after school. There were

three of them, slouching across the pavement
barring his way.

"It's the Jiminy Cricket," said one.

"Dirty Gyp," said another.

"Hand it over," said the third. "We know you pinched it. My new CD." Jim recognised him from class, a strapping boy with thick lips and pimples, and he knew it was no use saying he knew nothing. They made a grab at his sleeve.

"You pass it over – or else."

They jumped him, he dodged, then they were
all rolling on the ground, kicking and punching,
a mess of sweating armpits and flailing legs,
and he wished he was the camp dog, Towser, so
that he could give them a good bite where they'd
remember. His jacket was pulled open, they
yanked back his shoulder. His head hit the kerb, a
knee jammed his rib.

"Stop that!" someone shouted. They froze. His three tormentors picked themselves up. It was the chippie, who'd come out, waving his fist.

"You're a desperate pack, the lot of you. Git on with you."

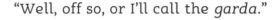

"Mr Kelly," the third one said. "We were only after something this tinker pinched."

"And did you find it?"

"No – but—"

"Well, off so, or I'll call the *garda*."

They straggled away. Jim slowly got to his feet.

"Are yous alright?" said the chippie.

"S'pose."

"D'you want some chips?

"That Cunningham lad's always causing trouble," the chippie said as the chips fizzled in their frying basket. "Like his drunken tyke of a father before him. The others are just his rag-tag-and-bobtails. There's good, middling and bad Buffers – but he's bad."

Jim started. "Buffers? So you're one of us?"

"Aye, lad. I was a Traveller once. Still am in my blood. I settled in Dundray as a young man when I found my Eileen. The best of Buffers, my Eileen. Bought a van and mooched a living from the burgers. Then we married and I got this shop. Here's your chips."

Jim poured the ketchup on. "Don't you miss it?" he said. "The travelling life?"

"What? The road, the backchat, the camp fires? Sometimes. But when it rains – then no, I'd as lief be here indoors, toasting my toes."

The door burst open and Kit came in, breathless.

"They're after you! Moss Cunningham and his gang."

"Don't I know it," said Jim. Her bunches had come down, her tie flapped over her shoulder and she looked as odd as a frog in pyjamas with her misshapen clothes and blotched skin.

"Have a chip," he said.

Before she could accept, a crowd came in, jostling at the counter.

"It's the tinker-wop again," said one. "Doesn't he follow you around like a bad smell?"

"I'm away," Jim muttered.

But Kit followed him down the pier.

"Were you really baptised six times,
Jim Curran?" she called after him.

He stopped to let her catch up.

"I dunno – Mam says the priests used to slip
a pound into the baby shawl after every baptism,
so she took me round the churches getting me
baptised at all the villages. But I think she's only
codding. That's Mam. You never know when she's
having a rise."

He offered her some chips and they munched
in silence.

"Do you like school?" Jim said.

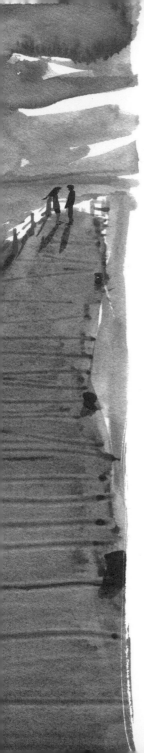

"My dad says I'm thicker than the kitchen table."

"What about your mam? What does she say?"

"She's dead. And don't be saying you're sorry."

"I wasn't. I was only going to say, 'God be Good to Her'. It's what we say whenever we mention the dead."

"God be Good to Her," said Kit, trying it out. "Are you a religious people, so?"

"Mam is. She slips into the church when it's quiet, before the tea. She sits alone in a pew and communes, like."

"Doesn't she go to mass?"

"Not her. She doesn't like the missals the Buffers hand out. She can't read, sees."

"She can't read?"

"No."

"Not a word?"

"No."

They reached the end of the pier.

"My dad's never out of church since my mam died," said Kit. "He does all the masses. He offers up ten novenas and swings the incense. He collects the money. You've probably seen him down Castle Street. Rattling his tin can."

"*He's* your da?"

"'Fraid so. Don't be going giving him anything, because you know what?"

"What?"

"He keeps the lot. Stuffs it in an old kettle under his bed."

"No!"

"He does so. And he never gives me any, the stingy devil. You see this uniform?" She plucked a fold of maroon material from her waist.

"Aye. You'd hardly miss it."

"Three sizes too big. A right tent. He says it will do till I leave school, it's a waste of money buying the right size."

"He's a stingy devil, all right."

They leaned against the rails, looking out to sea.

"Nothing between us and America," said Kit. "Wish I could swim across."

"I can't either," he said.

"You can't swim?"

"No. Read. I can't read." He waited to see if she would be surprised. "It's not just my mam. My da can't. My cousins can't. And nor me." He shook his head.

"Not even a bit?"

"Not a holy notion."

"Would you like to?"

Jim shrugged.

"I'm sure I could show you," she coaxed.

"Never."

"I could."

"All right so – but don't be telling."

There was a cave Kit knew, in the cliffs below the golf course. She said it was called Haggerty's Hellhole, but through a crack in the back was a larger

chamber, like a cathedral, with pillars and arches,

vaulting into darkness. It was a beautiful place,

she said, made from a million years of wind and

sea.

They met in there after school, on Kit's shopping days. She brought along a book from her childhood about ponies and gymkhanas by somebody with hyphens in their name. He didn't like it much, but he tried to read it just to please her. She read a sentence and he read it after her.

They used a torch to see the pages. But he relied more on memorising her words as they echoed around the cave than on what he saw in the round of light.

"Do you think I'm pretty, Jim?" she'd said once.

He'd shone the torch into her eyes, running it down over her mouse-like nose and chapped lips, and switched it off.

"You're all right in the right light," he'd said.

She squealed and clouted him, he'd tickled her under her arms and they'd ended up having a short kiss in the dark under the dripping stalactites. Then she'd sang him a song about a blacksmith who marries the wrong lassie, the one with the land and no heart. He lay against her and felt where the notes started and when she finished they kissed again.

"Where've you bin, Jimmy?" his da said when he got in, late.

"I went tramping on the cliffs," he replied. "I like the birds there."

"Aye, it's that time of year," his mam pitched in. "The skylarks are up. You can't see them but you can hear them."

"As long as it's only skylarks," said his da.

By the end of three weeks, his after-school meanderings resulted in six bruises, a bad rib and a swell on the cheekbone, courtesy of the Cunningham gang, and a few common pronouns and twenty-eight kisses, courtesy of Kit. In class, Mr Tassey seemed to go along with Jim's rendering of the Invisible Man. He ignored him.

At break, he joined the cousins in a schoolground corner and they swapped tales of Terror, Torture and Annihilation. May and Lil said their classes were full of gawps and goons, who kept away after they'd promised to put curses on anyone crossing their path. Declan never said much. He had the look of a pup with a sore toe pad and his spray came out every five minutes.

Moss Cunningham usually drifted over to deliver a few taunts with the rag-and-bobtailing gang. Lil and May would close their eyes and speak the Cant, cursing them under their tongues, while Jim blew on his knuckles.

"Just you wait, Jim Curran," said Moss. "We'll get that CD back. You're a pack of thieving bastards."

One of the gang, a girl, shook out her foxy hair and wrinkled her nose up. "I've a song for you, Jim Curran," she said.

"Jim Curran,

Stinks like the Burren,

Talks all foreign

Brains like a moron."

The teacher blew the whistle, which was just as well since Jim felt like splitting her lip.

"By tomorrow, or else," said Moss Cunningham. "If that CD's not back, you and your tinker cousins will know about it."

"What CD?" snapped May. "We don't even have a CD player."

That night, his mam stepped through the
string-bead curtain after he'd settled in his bunk.
The beads clacked after her and she turned down
the gas lamp. He
could see her in
the dusky light, her
face worn with the
day but smiling.

"How's school, Jimmy?"

"Same's ever. The pits."

"How're the teachers?"

"Same's ever. The pit donkeys."

"And how're the pupils?"

"The pit donkeys' monkeys."

"S'that so, Jimmy?"

"Aye."

"Only, I wondered. If maybe you'd a friend."

"Why d'you say that?"

She shrugged. "No reason. Just a notion. Have you any words of the reading picked up?"

He sat up. "One or two. I can read what it says on Da's stout."

"Even I know what that says." She leaned over and whispered. "If you learn a few words, could you ever pass them on to me?"

He stared at her and she reached out a hand to touch his head. He knew that she was blessing him, so he tried not to wriggle away.

When she'd done, she left softly through the beads and he lay staring up at the fish mobiles

spinning in slow motion from the ceiling. They'd made them together when he was small and they still hung over his pillow, spangling with carefree colours.

Later, he heard his mam and da talking when they thought he was asleep.

"Mirt's worried," his da said. "The asthma's worse. He's not eating. Or talking. He's like a silent movie."

"Declan was always delicate. Not like our Jim."

"We should take them all out of that school and have done with it. Buffer schools never did us Pavees any favours."

"I think our Jim's getting some words this time. You know that sign down by the cross? He told me what it says."

"What?"

"Castlebar, three miles."

"Even I knew that."

Jim smiled and turned over, drawing the patchwork around his ears. There was something

warm in his brain. The thought of Kit and the fishes and the new words was like bread rising with the yeast.

"Wisht," was the last thing he heard his mam say. "You'll wake that son of ours."

"POLICE, POLICE, OPEN UP."

He woke to thumps and trailer shudderings, dogs barking, lights flashing through the windows.

"God have mercy," said Mam.

"It's the *garda*," said Da. "Won't they ever give us peace?"

Jim jumped down from his bunk and hopped into his trousers.

"They're after us this time and no messing," he said. His da threw him a sour glance.

"Just you shut it, lad," he said. He opened the door and roared. "What the bloody heck—"

But they burst in, five of them, and they poked the blankets and scattered the shoes and rummaged the cupboards. His mam followed them round, with the rosary in both hands, saying the Hail Marys. Perhaps because of her, they left his fish mobile alone. They upended the pots and hurled the cushions and when they had finished ransacking, they threw the loose things – brasses, lamps, chairs, pictures, tins, baskets – out onto the grass. His mam's Virgin Mary statue broke in two.

"What're yous looking for?" Jim said.

They didn't reply. They moved on through the camp like locusts, leaving piles on the verge behind them.

"Fit to burn," said one. "A lot of stinking crap."

"What're yous looking for?" repeated Jim. His da and the other Pavees were a gathering of silent onlookers with grim faces. Jim wanted to scream, don't just stand there, stop them, but they stood stock still and said nothing. His da gripped Towser by the scruff of his neck. His dog snout pointed forwards, his teeth were bared. His body was a long, low growl.

"That your dog?" a policeman said.

"He's the camp dog," Jim's da said. "He belongs to us all."

"Then where is it?"

"Where's what?"

The man folded his arms, tut-tutting and shaking his head. He was plainclothes. Above a thin knotted tie, his throat bulged.

"As if you didn't know. The dog licence, of course."

Nobody said anything. There was just a hardening silence. Towser's growling stopped.

"We'll be back," said the plainclothes. "In seven days. With your eviction notice. I advise you to be gone beforehand. Or we'll have you up in court."

Jim stepped back into his trailer. His mam sat huddled on the bunk, her face immobile, the rosary hanging limp through her fingers.

"They're gone," he said. "It's all right, Mam."

He sat beside her.

"They came the night you were born," she said. "I was bent over with the pains and old Doll was with me, with the kettle of boiling water. They sent it flying and it splashed over my legs."

She put her arm around him. "They must have heard me yellin' the other side of County Cork, so help me God. But you came along anyhows, there was nothing to stop you. But they put me off my stride. You came along the wrong way round."

He didn't know what to say.

"That was the end of the children," she said. They sat together listening to the men's low voices seething outside. He saw the greyness of dawn creeping in through the crack in the door.

"Why do they hate us, Mam?" he said.

"They say we're the cursed people, son," she said. "They say we're from a long line of blacksmiths, the tinnies that the Romans bribed to make the three nails for the cross of Jesus."

The next day, before classes started, the Cunningham gang turned on Kit.

"Jelly on a plate,

Jelly on a plate,

Wibble-wobble, wibble-wobble,

Jelly on a plate," they chanted.

They had Kit in the middle of a ring-a-roses, with her tie askew and the buttons of her blouse undone. Moss Cunningham lashed her with a rope.

"Tinker-scuzz," he said. "That's what tinker girlfriends are, no better than muck themselves. If you don't get your boyfriend to hand over the CD, I'll tell your dad."

Jim ran over and dived straight for Moss's legs. The two went flying, fisting and thrusting, while the others stood around. But in two shakes the fight was over. A whistle blew.

Mr Tassey appeared from nowhere. One of Moss's pimples had splatted into blood and pus, and Jim's knuckles itched for a swipe at the others.

"Yous – yous—" he hissed. Moss folded his arms, like the smug policeman from the night before. Mr Tassey seized Jim's shoulder. "One more word," he said. "Cunningham. Go wipe your nose. Curran – come with me. I've seen this coming for days."

As he was frogmarched indoors, he craned back to see Kit. She was buttoning up her shirt with small shaking hands. He recognised the white, vacant look in her face. She was the image of Declan.

They meant it as a punishment, but Jim found it the best school day ever. He was sent to the school librarian, a woman with wavy red hair called Mrs MacKenna.

"D'you know how to shelve?" she said.

"I do," he said. "I put up shelves for me mam last spring. Da showed me."

Mrs MacKenna smiled. "Not that kind of shelving." She showed him the spine of a book and pointed out a code at the bottom. "Fic," she said. "Means fiction. Made-up stories."

"Aren't all stories made up?"

"So they are. But fiction's *more* made up. Supposedly. Fiction goes on the right, non-fiction on the left. Stick to the numbers, not the names, and you won't go far wrong."

He trundled off, pushing the bookcase-on-wheels, and picked through the books. He knew his numbers, now, and because of Kit he knew half his letters. Mrs MacKenna didn't get in his way and by noon he'd shelved them all.

During lunch, Mrs MacKenna let him sit in the last bay where nobody could see him. The Cunningham gang came in searching, but she shooed them away.

Then she gave him a book about birds in the British Isles. He turned the pages to a small brown bird sitting among the dunes. He looked at the black print beneath the picture and suddenly realised he could read it. *Skylark.*

He took a picture Kit had given him of herself and on the back he copied down the word: Skylark.

The next day, at break time, May and Lil said they were mitching off down the beach.

"Uncle Mirt says we can pack school in soon, anyways," said Lil.

"Where's Declan?" said Jim.

"Dunno."

He saw Kit come rushing over.

"Is that the girl they say you're goin' with?" said Lil. "She looks a right dumb-bell in those baggy clothes."

"You belt up," said Jim. "Or I'll tell about the fags you stole from my da."

May and Lil drifted away as Kit approached.

"Jimmy," she panted. "I overheard the gang in the cloakrooms. They're planning something for your Declan. They said something about Mrs MacKenna."

They looked around, but there was no sign of the gang.

"Whatever it is, I'd say they're doing it now," said Kit.

A terrible clarity unrolled in Jim's head. "The library," he said. "Mrs MacKenna said she's off today. It'll be deserted."

They ran indoors, up the stairs and in through the library's swing doors, but when they got there, all was still.

"Nothing," said Kit.

"Shh—"

There was a rasp from the back bay. He ran forwards and found Declan, spreadeagled across the table with rope pinioning his wrists and ankles to the legs. They had stuffed a sock in his mouth. His eyes were glassy, as if he wasn't there, his cheeks were the colour of the sea on a bad day. Jim pulled out the sock and he could hardly breathe himself.

He found Declan's spray in his pocket and yanked open his mouth. He squirted it in.

Kit started untying him.

"Yous leave him alone," Jim screamed,
pushing her away violently. She reeled against
another table. He gave another squirt on the
inhaler and couldn't see whether it worked

because his face was hot and his eyes filmed over. "Yous leave him," he wailed. "Yous keep yous dirty filthy Buffer fingers off him. Yous bastard Buffers, I'll pay you all out, yous—"

Declan rasped and writhed on the table, like a fish on the end of a line. There was a rattling in his throat as if the air was drowning him, then a terrible wheezing. A long droop of spittle came down his chin.

"Declan," Jim called. "Declan. Come back."

He found his penknife and cut the cords and picked the small boy up to help him breathe. Declan retched out a mix of phlegm and vomit. Jim held him in his arms as his mam had held him the night before. "Our Declan," he kept saying. "You're all right now." When he looked up, Kit had gone. Mr Tassey was there instead.

"Kit told me what happened," he said. "We've called an ambulance."

That night, Jim looked on as the men made a fire and stood around drinking stout. Declan was safe home from hospital, asleep in the top trailer, and they spoke low, as if not to disturb him.

"That's it," said Uncle Mirt. "That's the last time my Declan goes near that school."

"They've given us another eviction notice," Da said. "The summer's over before it's started in Dundray."

"Let's go," someone said.

"No," said another. "Let's stay."

They talked the back-and-fores-let's-goes-
let's-stays, while the moon rose over the hills into
the twilight, but Jim knew how it would end. It
always ended the same way.

"Our Shay got properly fixed in Inverness,"
said one. "He met a
Scottish lassie on the
road, and they stopped
at a grand site, water
on tap, and they're still
there with their three
wee ones."

"They've better sites
over the water."

"Better laws too."

Jim's mam came
over and pitched in.

"You men," she scolded. "You're all the same. The grass is always greener. You have your hopes. So you move on. Then your hopes go. You move on again. Is it never-ending? Can't we just for once stay and fight it out?"

Jim took Towser and wandered the hillside. It grew slowly darker. It wasn't properly night until gone eleven, up north. When the first star appeared, he turned back. The men had gone inside, but his mam still stood by the embers in her tweed coat.

"The men have decided," she said wearily. "No more school. We're packing up tomorrow and moving on."

"Where to?"

"East to Larne for the boat. We're leaving Ireland, son. We're crossing the water. But what good'll come of it, I don't know."

He waited in the cave next afternoon, while
they packed up the camp. Would she come, or
wouldn't she? He blew brash noises from the
grasses he'd picked on the clifftop, and the
cave laughed them back, and he thought of the
skylarks he'd spotted, and wished he hadn't
pushed her. *Would she or wouldn't she?*

She came in with a Coke bottle for him and a smile.

"There you are," she said.

"There you are," he repeated. He couldn't help grinning from ear to ear.

"We're like Romeo and Juliet," she said.

"Romeo and Juliet?" he mimicked in a la-di-dah voice.

"We read it last term. It wasn't bad."

"Hate that crap."

"Their families hate each other. They marry in secret. And then they both die."

"Sounds hilarious."

She passed him the Coke and he opened it with his knife. They sat close together on his jacket. "We're going, Kit," he said. "We're moving on. Tonight." He took her hand. "Across the water. They're evicting us."

"I knew it," she wailed. "When you all didn't show at school – I knew it."

He drank a little and they sat in silence. "Sing us a song," he said. "One last time."

Her voice, a pure and lovely thing, filled the vast space. The notes knocked around the walls, colliding together.

She sang the school hymn, but in the
cathedral chamber it sounded magnificent, with

the Love Divine coming up, down and around and
landing in his Pavee soul.

"What's it really like being a Traveller, Jim?"
she said afterwards.

He thought for a moment. "Da says
it's like being a fox instead of a dog," he said. "You
Buffers are the dogs, well-fed, well-trained, and
we're the roving foxes, lean and free."

"D'you like it?"

"Dunno. I just like being me."

He offered her a swig of Coke.

"My da," he said, "used to tell me about this
old black-and-white film, with the two tramps,
Stan and Ollie their names were, and they're in
France, sees, and the fat one, Ollie, loves a girl
who just laughs at him, so he decides to drown
himself. He goes off down the river to throw
himself in. But he brings the skinny one with him,

ties them together with rope, so's they can jump together, but before they jump the skinny one says, 'Do you believe in reincarnation?' And Ollie says, 'Why yes, I do.' The skinny one asks, 'What would you like to come back as?' 'A horse,' says Ollie, 'and what about you?' And you know what Stan says?"

"What?"

"Stan says, 'Gee, Ollie, I'd like to come back as me. I've had a swell time being me.'"

"What happens then?" said Kit. "Do they drown?"

"Nah. They jump in, but the water only reaches their knees."

The words of his story settled back into the dark places of the cave and he could feel Kit was crying, not laughing.

"Oh, Jim," she blurted. "I'll miss you when you go. I don't have a swell time being me."

"That's not true, Kit. Every time you sing you have a great time. I can see it in your eyes."

He leaned over and blew into her face. Her feather-duster fringe rose softly. He put her small hand under his armpit to keep it warm. He turned off the torch and they lay in the dark listening to the strange sound of the surf outside.

"The tide's coming in," she said. "Our clothes will be ruined."

"We could wait. Wait to see if we'd drown. Like Stan and Ollie."

"Never."

"We might."

"And would you be reincarnated? And come back as yourself?"

"Maybe. But I wouldn't mind being a nice dog, whatever Da says. Running around after the sheep, the boss of the farm. Chasing car tyres, getting my strokes at night. What would you come back as?"

"Dunno. Not me. Not a dog. Maybe as my mam."

"Your mam?"

"She was pretty. And funny. I'd come back as my mam but knowing not to marry my dad. I'd have a whole other life."

"When you're reincarnated, you forget everything. You'd probably marry your da all over again."

"I wouldn't!"

"You would so." He tickled her until she screeched.

"It would be nice in a way," she said after he stopped. "To stay here. Fall asleep maybe. And drown."

"We wouldn't though. The sea doesn't come in this far. We'd be like Stan and Ollie. Two damp squibs."

They lay for a while longer, but his da's accordion must have been quickstepping again because when Kit looked at her watch she leaped up.

"My dad'll be frantic for his supper."

Outside, the evening was clear and quiet. Before they parted she flung the empty Coke bottle out into the bright water.

"It will come back one day," she said. "Probably when we're so old we'll have forgotten it."

"I won't forget."

"Nor me," said Kit.

He took from his pocket a stone, black and round like a glossy egg, which he'd chosen for her on the beach. "It's yours," he said. "A real Dundray beauty."

She pressed it up to her cheek, and before she could say anything, he sprinted off along the beach towards the town.

Halfway to the pier he slowed to look back. He could see her, silhouetted against the fine sky, not having moved from where he had said goodbye. *Goodbye*, he said again in his head. He waved. Maybe she could still see him, maybe not, but even when he turned away, he could still see her.

He walked slowly back up to the camp, where
all their Dundray life was being folded away into
the trailers, and where the road beckoned again,
the road from their troubles, down to the cross,
up through the mountains, over to the other
side of Ireland and on to more troubles, the road
to Larne with its ferries sailing off to another
country.

"Thought you weren't
coming," Da said. "Where've
you bin?"

"Never mind our Jim,"
Mam said, throwing the wink.
"If I know him, he was away
over the cliffs, saying
goodbye to his
skylarks."

With thanks to the residents of the Wetlands Halting Site, Kilkenny. And to Paula Leyden and Children's Books Ireland for their support.

WHAT WE CALL OURSELVES, AND WHAT OTHERS CALL US — A NOTE ON THE WORD "PAVEE"

For much of her professional life, Siobhan Dowd worked to promote the rights of marginalised people and particularly travelling communities in England and Ireland. These communities are not homogenous groups and nor are they well understood, largely because they tend to be poorly represented and rarely have a voice in wider society. They are often called derogatory names. In this story Jim is called a "tinker" and a "gyp", with intent to offend. Today, council documents, the press and so on use new formal terms, created to address discrimination or promote respect. "Traveller" and "Gypsy/Traveller" are such terms. Many individuals do not identify themselves with these terms. These terms may also suggest links between disparate peoples that have never existed.

When Siobhan wrote this story, she drew on her own experience and that of her friendship circles within travelling communities. She chose the word "Pavee" for Jim to describe himself. This term is not uncommon in Ireland, but nor is it standard. It is a term a person may use to describe him or herself, but may object to if it is used by someone who does not belong to their community.

"Pavee" may come from the word "purvey", and may originally have meant an itinerant salesperson. "Tinker" has a similar root — in the word "tinsmith" — but is largely seen as derogatory today. The word "Pavee" may also offend some people, but Siobhan was confident that it belonged in the story she wrote, and she wrote that story as a tribute to the communities she worked so hard to serve and in which she had many friends.

THE AUTHOR

The Pavee and the Buffer Girl was Siobhan Dowd's first published fiction. She went on to win over 65 awards for her four books, including the Branford Boase Award for *A Swift Pure Cry*, and the Carnegie Medal and Bisto Award for *Bog Child*, published after her death. Before her writing career, Siobhan worked in human rights, particularly for writers' freedoms, and for the rights of children and travelling people. She died at the age of 47 in 2007.

THE ARTIST

Emma Shoard is an illustrator and printmaker from Brighton, who now lives in London on a barge on the Thames. Emma works mainly in ink, charcoal and pencil to create drawings that capture movement and purpose through free and fast mark-making. *The Pavee and the Buffer Girl* is Emma's first graphic novel. To capture Jim and Kit's world, Emma spent time with families in the Wetlands Halting Site in Kilkenny with their friend and champion, the writer Paula Leyden, and visited caves, cliffs and other special places around Ireland.

THE SIOBHAN DOWD TRUST

Siobhan's legacy includes the Siobhan Dowd Trust, set up by Siobhan in her last days to give disadvantaged young people the opportunity to read and enjoy literature. The money earned through royalties and foreign sales of Siobhan's books allows the Trust to support deserving projects to take stories to children and young people without stories. The Trust's funding process is open and flexible, which has enabled many groups to develop fantastic projects across the UK and Ireland. Find out more at www.siobhandowdtrust.com.